10 Minute Classics

Good books are some of the greatest treasures in the world. They can take you to incredible places and on fantastic adventures. So sit back with a 10 MINUTE CLASSIC and indulge a lifelong love for reading.

We cannot, however, guarantee your 10 minute break won't turn into 15, 20, or 30 minutes, as these FUN stories and engaging pictures will have you turning the pages AGAIN and AGAIN!

W9-CYS-147

Designed by Flowerpot Press
in Franklin, TN.
www.FlowerpotPress.com
Designer: Stephanie Meyers
Editor: Katrine Crow
ROR-0811-0117
ISBN: 978-1-4867-1271-7
Made in China/Fabriqué en Chine

The ADVENTURES of TOM SAWYER

Mark Twain

Retold by Dan Gibson
with Illustrations by Asha Pearse

The Adventures of Tom Sawyer is a story that took place way back when America was still growing west, and the land was a little wild and full of adventure. It is the story of a boy who was a lot like that land and time.

Tom Sawyer lived with his Aunt Polly in a small town on the Mississippi River. He was clever and mischievous, which can be a potent combination. Mischief often landed Tom *in* trouble. Cleverness often helped Tom *out* of trouble.

And there was quite a bit of trouble…

...like the time Tom snuck into Aunt Polly's pantry and swiped a jar of her prize-winning jam, even though he had been warned not to touch it.

To make matters worse, Tom then outwitted Aunt Polly, sneaking away before she knew what was happening. He was a rascal alright, but his Aunt Polly loved Tom so dearly she could hardly bring herself to punish him.

One day, Tom played hooky* from school and got up to all sorts of shenanigans. By the time he arrived home, Aunt Polly was fit to be tied. When she tried to get Tom to admit he had skipped school, he cleverly avoided her questioning. Then he escaped into town…only to get into a fight with a "city boy." *(Not to worry, Tom cleverly got the better of him.)*

When Tom again returned home, this time ragged and dirty, Aunt Polly told him he would be spending his Saturday whitewashing their fence as punishment.

It sure did hurt to be mischievous.

*(Being an obedient child, you probably do not even know that playing "hooky" means missing school without permission.)

That Saturday, Tom's unsuspecting friends came by for a visit. They all teased him for not getting to go swimming. Tom ignored the teasing and instead acted as if whitewashing a fence was the most fun thing in the world.

One by one, Tom convinced his friends that he was very lucky to *get* to whitewash a fence. In no time at all, they were begging for a turn. Tom acted reluctant, which just made his friends want a turn even more, and soon his pals were *paying* him to *let* them have a turn whitewashing! When they didn't have money, Tom took their favorite trinkets as payment.

Instead of suffering through punishment, Tom Sawyer spent that Saturday lounging in the sun while his *friends* finished *his* chores. By the end of the day he was rich, with pockets filled with marbles, an apple, a mouth harp, a kite, and many other prized possessions.

It sure did pay to be clever.

There was one boy in town who would not fall for Tom's tricks. That boy was Tom's best friend and adventuring pal, Huckleberry Finn. Huck Finn had a tough life, but Huck said he liked it that way. Tom and Huck shared many big adventures...

The two friends often went on treasure hunts, all the while discussing what they would do with the treasure once it was theirs. Huck decided he would spend his share of the loot on pie and soda while Tom said he would probably use his share to settle down and get married.

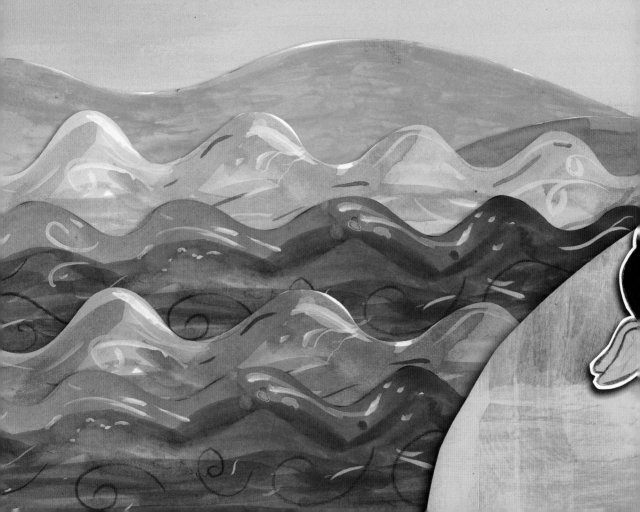

Tom and Huck also loved to explore secret caves. There, they would find waterfalls, stalactites, hidden passageways, and, on one occasion, a whole mess of bats. The bats startled the boys so much that Tom ran the wrong way and got lost in the cave. For three days, Tom rationed the sweets he'd stashed in his pockets, until finally he was found and rescued.

One night, while exploring the local cemetery, Tom and Huck stumbled on some bad guys and even witnessed a murder! When the wrong person ended up being accused of the murder, Tom wasn't sure what to do. Though Huck told him to stay quiet, that just didn't sit right with Tom.

Despite being scared, Tom couldn't stand the idea of someone getting in trouble for something they didn't do, so he rustled up his bravery and told the truth. Huck saw Tom was thinking about someone other than himself when he did this, something Huck wasn't used to doing, and he admired it and made note of it.

It sure felt good to be brave.

One day, Tom and Huck decided to sneak away and take an adventure to Jackson Island, a small patch of land about three miles downriver. They took a raft and a pole and set off. The friends pretended to be pirates as they navigated the waterway.

Once they arrived at the island, Tom and Huck spent time fishing, cooking stolen bacon over a campfire, and discussing how exactly pirates were supposed to act. It was a grand time! They fell asleep with their heads full of adventure.

Unfortunately, the part-time pirates awoke the next morning to find their raft had drifted away. They were stranded on the island with no way home. A bit of homesickness began to tug at them.

Soon, the boys heard the faint sound of their names being called and realized people were looking for them. As it turned out, their capsized boat had been found near town and the boys had been presumed dead. Everyone was preparing for their funeral! Everyone was preparing for their funeral!

Not too many boys get to witness their own funeral…

Tom and Huck decided it would be fun to hide out in the gallery of the church to see how their funeral service went. Before it was over, they couldn't find a dry eye in the house—not even their own. When Tom and Huck came out of hiding and walked down the aisle wiping their tears, the church was in shock—especially Aunt Polly. She could not decide whether to give Tom a cuff or a kiss, so she did both!

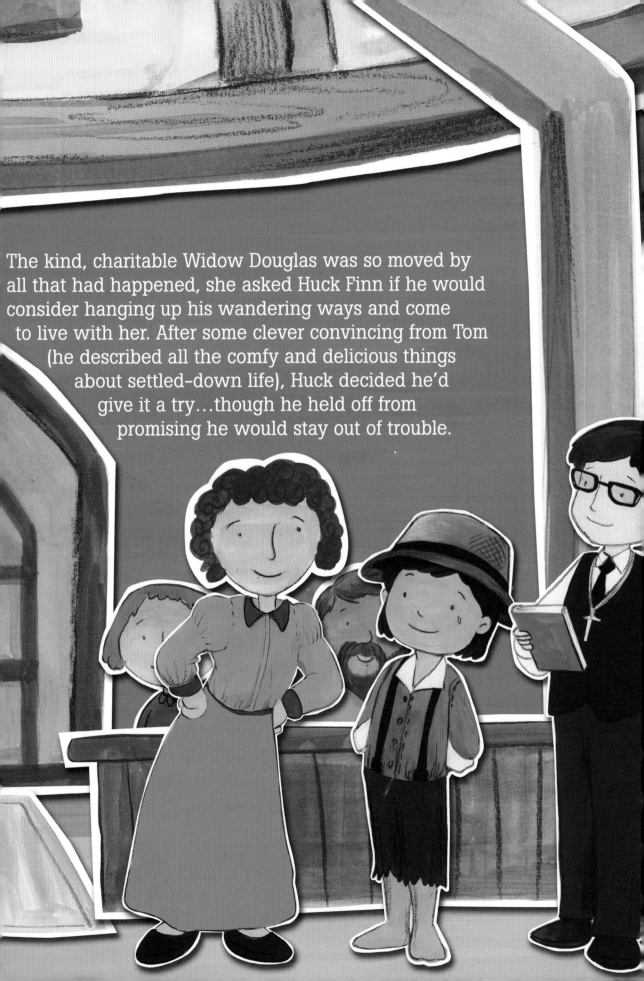

The kind, charitable Widow Douglas was so moved by all that had happened, she asked Huck Finn if he would consider hanging up his wandering ways and come to live with her. After some clever convincing from Tom (he described all the comfy and delicious things about settled-down life), Huck decided he'd give it a try...though he held off from promising he would stay out of trouble.

Tom and Huck had many more adventures and misadventures. It seemed that every time their love of mischief led them into trouble, their cleverness led them back out. It was how they loved to live.

And if you'd love to read more about it,
you should check out another fun book.
It's called *The Adventures of Huckleberry Finn*!